For Charlie
– C.F.

For Gwen the hen (R.I.P.)
and a very special little piglet, Ella Rose
– L.S.

E
FRE

SIMON AND SCHUSTER
First published in Great Britain in 2006 by Simon & Schuster UK Ltd
Africa House, 64-78 Kingsway, London WC2B 6AH

Book designed by Genevieve Webster
The text for this book is set in Cochin
The illustrations are rendered in watercolour

A CIP catalogue record for this book is available
from the British Library upon request

ISBN 0-689-87307-7
EAN 9780689873072
Printed in China
1 3 5 7 9 10 8 6 4 2

Squabble and Squawk

Claire Freedman & Leonie Shearing

SIMON AND SCHUSTER
London New York Sydney

Piglet and Yellow Hen were very best friends.

They did everything together.

They played peepo amongst the haystacks.

They raced around the farmyard, playing chase.

And on rainy days they sat in the old barn,
and told each other funny jokes.

One sunny day, Piglet wanted to play catch,
but Yellow Hen said she would rather make daisy chains.

"It's not fair!" cried Piglet. "We always do what you want!"
"We don't!" Yellow Hen replied. "I never get to choose!"

Their disagreement became a squabble. The squabble became
an argument and the argument bubbled over into a huge row.

The other farm animals came running to see
what all the squabbling and squawking was about.
"We can't have you two falling out!" said Sheep and Duck.
"No, we can't," agreed Horse. "Say sorry and make up."

"Yellow Hen should say sorry first," Piglet shouted.

"She started it."

"I did not," Yellow Hen squawked, stamping her little feet.

"I never want to be Piglet's friend, ever again."

The situation went from bad to terrible.
Soon Piglet and Yellow Hen stopped speaking to each other.
It was as if a big, black rain cloud had settled over
the farmyard and it was making everyone feel glum.

"I can't stand this," sighed Cow. "My milk will turn sour!"
"And I don't enjoy quacking like I used to," said Duck.
Everyone decided they had to get Piglet and Yellow Hen
back together again, for the good of the farm.

The next day, Sheep and Duck were walking past the milking shed when they spotted one of Farmer Barrow's gloves. It gave them a clever idea.

"We'll need to stick on some feathers," said Duck excitedly, "to make it more life-like!"
"And paint on a face," Sheep giggled.
"Let's go and tell Cow and Horse our plan!"

"What a great idea!" said Horse. "I'll find the crate."

"And I'll get some black paint," mooed Cow.

"Remember," whispered Duck, "we mustn't let Piglet or
Yellow Hen guess what we're up to . . ."

The next morning Piglet was sitting all alone in his pigsty, feeling sorry for himself, when Sheep rushed over in an absolute panic.

"It's Yellow Hen!" she cried. "Farmer Barrow has stuffed
her in a big crate and he's going to take her to market!
Save her, Piglet, *save her*!"

"Oh no!" gasped Piglet. "It can't be true!" His heart
thumpity-thumped. He forgot his row with Yellow Hen
and raced across the farmyard.

It was true! A large crate was tied to Farmer Barrow's
truck and poor Yellow Hen was trapped inside.
Piglet could just see her feathers between the wooden slats.

"Don't worry, Yellow Hen," yelled Piglet. "I'll save you!"
With a mighty cry, he leapt onto the truck.

He tugged and tugged at the crate, but it wouldn't open.
"Breathe in, Yellow Hen!" puffed Piglet . . .

. . . as he pulled her out by her tail feathers.

Bump! The pair landed in a huge heap of sawdust.

The other animals rushed over, and first on the scene was –
to Piglet's amazement – *Yellow Hen*!

"Oh, Piglet!" she clucked, hugging him tight. "I ran here as soon as Duck told me you were being taken to market."
"But . . ." puffed a confused Piglet. "That's impossible! I've just pulled you out of this crate."

Then they both looked at the yellow feathery thing
half-buried in the sawdust.
"It's one of Farmer Barrow's gloves," spluttered Piglet.
The other animals tried hard not to laugh.

"It looks like we've been tricked," said Yellow Hen.
"I should have guessed!" giggled Piglet. "After all,
Farmer Barrow would never send us to market – he only
takes cabbages and tomatoes."

"I've missed you," said Yellow Hen.

"Me too," said Piglet. "Let's never squabble again!"

"Never, ever!" Yellow Hen smiled as they linked arms.

Cow and Horse cheered happily.
"That old glove trick worked a treat!" laughed Duck.
"One of my better plans!"

"*Excuse me,*" said Sheep. "That glove trick was my idea."

"You silly thing!" Duck quacked. "It was mine."

"It was not!" scoffed Sheep.

"Oh no," cried the animals. "Not again!"

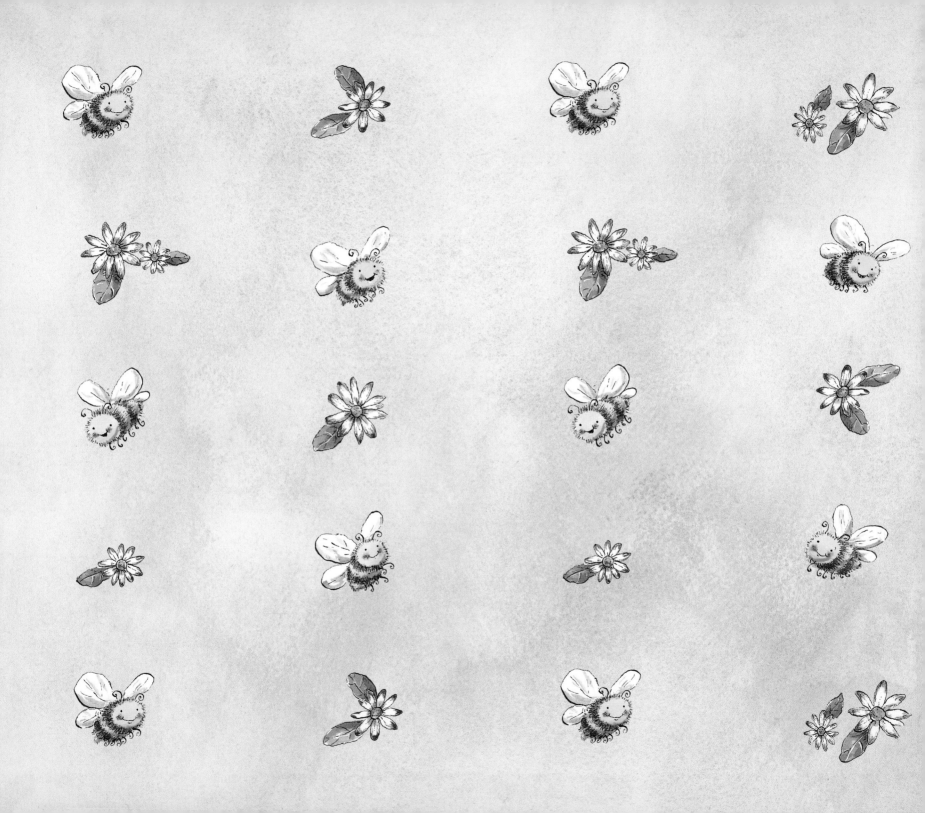